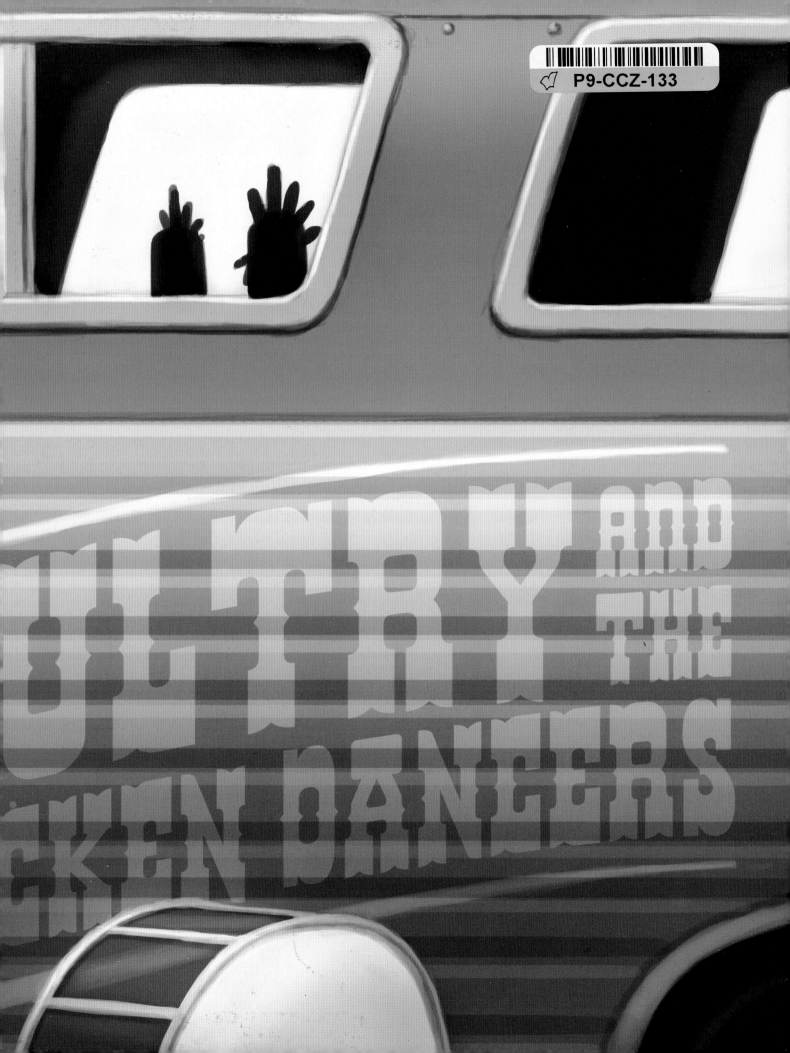

The challenge?
A talent contest!

What talent to show off?
Tightrope walking was out.

The competition
was fierce . . .

. . . and kept on coming.

FOR FRANCES: MUCH! – T.S.   TO ALEK, KYLE, AND LEAH – D.S.

STERLING CHILDREN'S BOOKS and the distinctive Sterling Children's Books logo are trademarks of Sterling Publishing Co., Inc.
Published by Sterling Publishing Co., Inc., 387 Park Avenue South, New York, NY 10016.

© 2012 by Tammi Sauer   Illustrations © 2012 by Dan Santat

All rights reserved. No part of this publication may be reproduced, stored in a retrieval system, or transmitted, in any form or by any
means, electronic, mechanical, photocopying, recording, or otherwise, without prior written permission from the publisher.

ISBN 978-1-4027-7837-7 (print format)

Distributed in Canada by Sterling Publishing, c/o Canadian Manda Group, 165 Dufferin Street, Toronto, Ontario, Canada M6K 3H6.
Distributed in the United Kingdom by GMC Distribution Services, Castle Place, 166 High Street, Lewes, East Sussex, England BN7 1XU.
Distributed in Australia by Capricorn Link (Australia) Pty. Ltd., P.O. Box 704, Windsor, NSW 2756, Australia.

For information about custom editions, special sales, and premium and corporate purchases,
please contact Sterling Special Sales at 800-805-5489 or specialsales@sterlingpublishing.com.

Manufactured in China.
Lot #:
2 4 6 8 10 9 7 5 3 1
11/11

www.sterlingpublishing.com/kids

But our Chicken Dance ROCKED!

We didn't win the contest . . .
but we were winners in Elvis Poultry's eyes.
(Where ARE his eyes?)

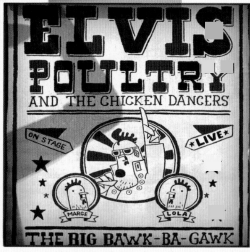

Ta-da! — Now we're on tour!
Wonder what will happen next!

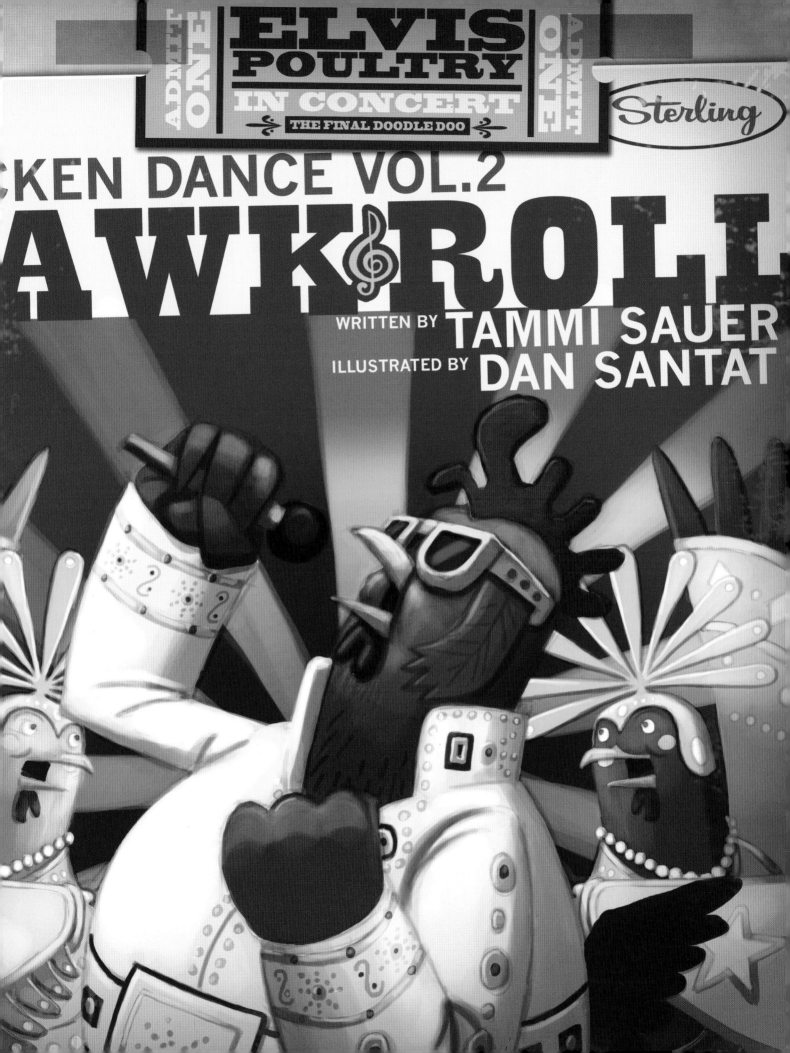

Marge and Lola leaned out the tour bus window.

"We'll miss you!" they called.

Their barnyard buddies waved.

"Good luck on your tour! Write to us!"

"We love you, chickens!"

Elvis lowered his shades.

"C'mon, chicks. Let's roll."

Marge and Lola settled into their seats,
and the bus rumbled down the road.

The first stop was McDoodle's Barnyard.

Elvis Poultry and the Chicken Dancers took the stage.
The lights went down.
The curtains went up.
The barnyard went wild.

"Wow," said Marge. "That's a big crowd."

"Woah," said Lola. "And we don't know *anyone.*"

The chickens trembled. They fanned their wattles. They . . .

"The next gig will be better," said Elvis. "Just chill, chicks."
"I know!" said Marge. "Let's picture the crowd in their *underwear.*"
"Tightie whities?" Lola nodded. "That should work."
But . . .

Lola sighed. "Maybe we should just ease into the next show."
"Ease into it?" asked Elvis. "That's a rockin' idea."

"I don't think this is what she had in mind," said Marge.

Elvis glided to the stage.

And the chickens?

Marge and Lola tried new ways to calm their jitters.

But nothing worked.
"We'll try one more show," said Elvis.
"If our flock can't rock, I gotta go solo."

That night, Marge and Lola felt smaller than chicken feed.
"I don't get it," said Lola. "We've got style. We've got rhythm.
What are we missing?"

Then Marge grinned.
"We're missing the most important thing of all!"

The chickens crossed the road.

They knew just what to do.

The next evening, the tour bus rolled into Dale's Dairy Farm.
Marge and Lola zipped backstage and peered through the curtains.

Their feathers drooped.

"This doesn't look good," said Lola.

"We're going to get mooed off the stage," said Marge.

Then the lights went down.
The curtains went up.
The cow crowd went wild.

Elvis! Elvis! Elvis!

The chickens trembled.
They fanned their wattles.
They . . .

. . . heard some very familiar voices.

"*We love you, chickens!*"
In the stands were some very familiar faces.
"They got our letter," whispered Lola.
"And we've got the best friends ever," said Marge.
The chickens faced the crowd. "Hey, Dale's Dairy Farm!"
called Lola. "Let's see your *moooooooves!*"

Everyone got in the moo-d.

Elvis was so inspired, he came up with a brand new song.
"Thank you. Thank you very much."
Marge and Lola gave each other a high five.

ARGE AND LOLA
AKE, RATTLE, AND ROLL

BAWk—BAWk—BAWk—BAWk

Barnyard100

Ever since, the chickens were bona fide superstars.
There was only one thing that Marge and Lola loved more than all the fame . . .

This Week	Last Week	Two Weeks Ago	Weeks On Chart	Title, Artist Imprint / Catalog No. / Distributing Label
1	1	1	10	Blue Moo, Elvis Poultry
2	4	8	6	It's Raining Milk, Colonel Cluck
3	7	23	7	The Sheeps Dig Me, MC Baas - A - Lot

... their fan club.